HÄGAR

THE HORRIBLE

SACKING PARIS ON A BUDGET

by DIK BROWNE

Volume II of
THE BEST OF HÄGAR THE HORRIBLE

TOR

A TOM DOHERTY ASSOCIATES BOOK

Sacking Paris on a Budget is a selection
of cartoons taken from *The Best of Hagar
the Horrible*, originally published by
Simon and Schuster in May 1981.

A Tom Doherty Associates Book

A TOR BOOK

Printed in the United States of America
Distributed by Pinnacle Books, Inc.

9 8 7 6 5 4 3 2

THE CURE

THE CHALLENGE

EVERY WORD IS TRUE

DO YOU HAVE TO START EVERY DAY YELLING IT AT THE TOP OF YOUR LUNGS ?!!

BIG FAT FRIEND

HEY! ISN'T IT TIME FOR MY AFTERNOON SNACK?!

NO

I'M ON A DIET

FLAVORS OF LOVE

THE EVIL OMEN

HAGAR'S RECIPE

THE BATTLE

TOO WELCOME

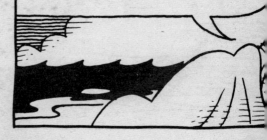

LISTEN TO THE NOISE
THAT STUPID SEA
IS MAKING!

I CAN'T SLEEP WITH THAT
LAP, LAP, LAPPING OF THOS
DUMB WAVES — *I'M
GONNA STOP IT!*

PERSONALITY

HANDS OFF!

YOU KNOW.... FOR A LADIES' DRINK, IT HAS A PRETTY GOOD KICK.

THE INVASION

NATIVE GAMES

SPEED READER

HOMECOMING

NAME DROPPER

GEE, HAGAR... I DON'T THINK WE'RE STRONG ENOUGH TO TAKE ON A CASTLE!

EVEN A DUMP LIK THAT...

OKAY! SURRENDER! COME ON OUT WITH YOUR HANDS UP!

THOSE NORMANS NEVER KNEW WHAT HIT THEM!

AT LAST! THE FIRES OF HOME! I HAVEN'T HAD A WARM MEAL SINCE WE LEFT TO RAID NORMANDY!

THE PROMPTER

TROOP MORALE

THE SUMMONS

ANSWER MAN

WHEN I GET OUT OF THIS, THERE'S GOING TO BE ONE DEAD GHOSTWRITER!

BAG ONE FOR M
BRING BACK SOMETHING LIGHT FOR DINNER—LIKE A BULL MOOSE—AN MAKE SURE IT'S TENDER AND NOT TOO FATTY.
ARE YOU SURE YOU KNOW THE MATING CALL OF THE BULL MOOSE?

DEAR DEBATER

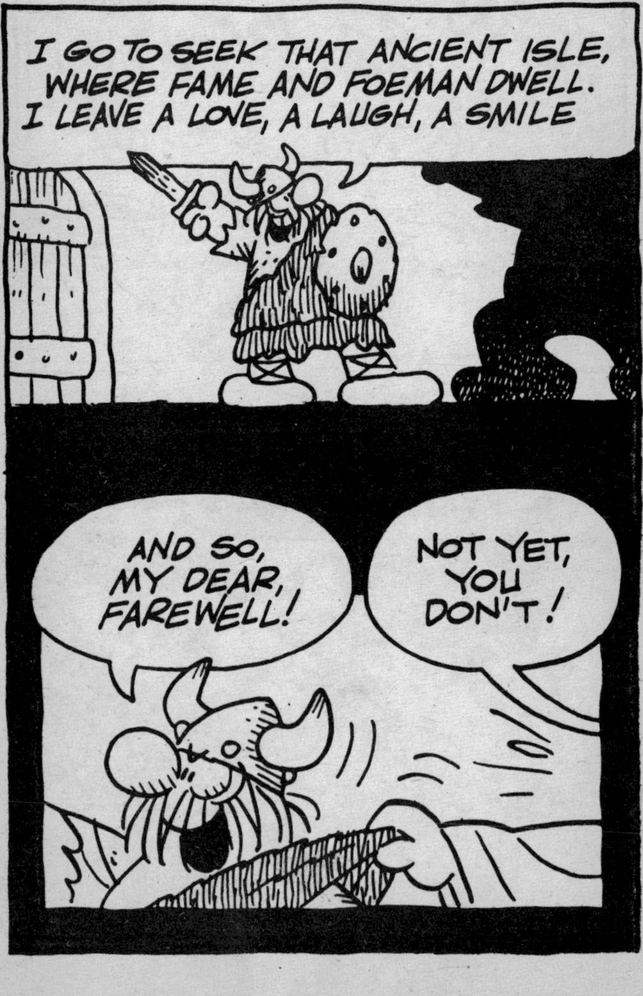

TABLE MANNERS

THE QUESTION

HAZARD DUTY